# KAY THOMPSON'S ELOISE
# Eloise and the Very Secret Room

STORY BY **Ellen Weiss**

ILLUSTRATED BY **Tammie Lyon**

Ready-to-Read

Simon Spotlight

New York    London    Toronto    Sydney    New Delhi

SIMON SPOTLIGHT

An imprint of Simon & Schuster Children's Publishing Division

1230 Avenue of the Americas, New York, NY 10020

First Simon Spotlight hardcover edition September 2016

First Aladdin Paperbacks edition October 2006

SIMON SPOTLIGHT, READY-TO-READ, and colophon are registered
trademarks of Simon & Schuster, Inc.

For information about special discounts for bulk purchases, please contact Simon & Schuster
Special Sales at 1-866-506-1949 or business@simonandschuster.com.

The text of this book was set in Century Old Style.

Manufactured in the United States of America 0816 LAK

2 4 6 8 10 9 7 5 3 1

The Library of Congress has cataloged a previous edition as follows:

Library of Congress Cataloging-in-Publication Data

Weiss, Ellen, 1949–

Eloise and the very secret room / story by Ellen Weiss ; illustrated by Tammie
Lyon. — 1st Aladdin Paperbacks ed.

p. cm. — (Kay Thompson's Eloise) (Ready-to-read)

"Based on the art of Hilary Knight" — P. [1]

Summary: Eloise discovers the Plaza Hotel's Lost and Found
and decides to make it her secret playroom.

[1. Lost and found possessions—Fiction. 2. Plaza Hotel (New York, N.Y.)—Fiction.
3. Hotels, motels, etc.—Fiction. 4. Humorous stories.] I. Lyon, Tammie, ill.
II. Thompson, Kay, 1911– III. Knight, Hilary, ill. IV. Title. V. Series.
VI. Series: Ready-to-read.

PZ7.W4475Elo 2006

[E]—dc22

2005029648

ISBN 978-1-4814-6750-6 (hc)

ISBN 978-0-689-87450-5 (pbk)

My name is Eloise.
I am six.

I live on
the tippy-top floor
of The Plaza Hotel.

But I can go all over.

This is Skipperdee.
He wears sneakers.
Sometimes.

Skipperdee and I
like to take walks.

Here is what I like to do:
go down
that very, very,
long, long hall.

(It is the one that
goes past the room
with the stringy mops.)

There is a room
that is so secret
only I know about it.

Skipperdee and I, anyway.

It says LOST AND FOUND.

Maybe it is lost,
but I found it.

There are very good things
in it.

If you tie a lot of
ties together,
you can jump rope.

It is also a good room
to spin in.

If we get tired,
we take a nap on a
fur coat.

Here is what else I can do:
wear nineteen hats.

A tennis racket makes
a very good turtle carrier.

I do not think anyone
has ever been in
this room but me.

It is a good room
to practice hollering in.

A hatbox makes a very good drum.

In comes Nanny.
"Eloise!" she says.
"Here you are!"

In comes the manager.
"Eloise!" he says.
"Here you are!"

"Of course I am here,"
  I say.
"Where else would I be?"

"We found you
in the Lost and Found,"
says Nanny.

I was not lost at all.
I was right here
all the time.
Oooooooo I love, love, love
the Lost and Found.

Tomorrow I will see if that hat makes a good fishbowl.